Joe and Sparky
Get New Wheels

Joe and Sparky
Get New Wheels

Jamie Michalak

illustrated by Frank Remkiewicz

CANDLEWICK PRESS

For my sister,
Queen Julie Boolie Pasta Fazooli.
It was all her idea.
J. M.

For Zack and Alex
F. R.

Text copyright © 2009 by Jamie Michalak
Illustrations copyright © 2009 by Frank Remkiewicz

First paperback edition in this format 2013

Library of Congress Cataloging-in-Publication Data is available.

Library of Congress Catalog Card Number 2008933675

ISBN 978-0-7636-3387-5 (hardcover)
ISBN 978-0-7636-6641-5 (paperback)

18 APS 10 9 8 7 6 5

Printed in Humen, Dongguan, China

This book was typeset in Adobe Caslon.
The illustrations were done in watercolor and colored pencil.

Candlewick Press
99 Dover Street
Somerville, Massachusetts 02144

visit us at www.candlewick.com

Contents

CHAPTER ONE
The Big Prize 1

CHAPTER TWO
Another Prize for Joe 13

CHAPTER THREE
Welcome to Tasty Burger 23

CHAPTER FOUR
On the Road 31

CHAPTER ONE
The Big Prize

In Safari Land, the famous cageless zoo, a turtle hid in his shell.

Not far away, a giraffe stretched his neck to see the world.

"It is here! It is here!" Joe Giraffe cheered.

"What is the hubbub?" Sparky asked, poking his head out of his shell.

"Do you remember the contest I entered?"

"Of course," said Sparky. "You found the paper on the ground. You wrote your name on it. You put the paper in the mailbox."

"Do you remember the prize?"

"Yes. You talked about it for weeks."

"I won!" Joe shouted. "I won the big prize! There it is at the end of the road."

"Giraffes do not win big prizes."

"Some do," said Joe.

"I do not see your big prize," Sparky said. "I see your big feet."

"You do not see much. That is the trouble with stumpy necks."

"Can you give me a lift?" asked Sparky.

"Always, my small, green friend."

Joe lowered his head. Sparky climbed
on top. Joe ran.

"SLOW DOWN! SAFETY FIRST!"
Sparky yelled.

But Joe did not like slow. He ran as fast
as he could.

At the end of the road was the Safari Land office. There was a lady with a green dress. There was a fancy car with no roof.

"There it is!" Joe said. "My bright yellow Super Flash 5000."

"It is bright," Sparky agreed.

Joe looked in the car. On the seat was a hat covered with fruit.

"Slam dunk! I won a hat, too!" Joe said.

He put Sparky on the seat.

"Is that a hat or is it lunch?" Sparky asked.

Joe put on the hat. He got into the car.

"We will go on a road trip," Joe said.

"Only if it is very short. And very slow," Sparky said. "Safety first!"

Joe started the car and drove to the gate.

"How do you know how to drive?" Sparky asked. "How do you know about contests and Super Flash 5000s?"

"I like to listen. I like to stretch my neck and see the world."

"I like to hide in my shell," said Sparky.
Suddenly, **BOOM! BANG!**
The Super Flash 5000 came to a halt.

"We are at the gate now," said Joe.
"You are a good driver, Joe. You know
how to stop," Sparky said.

The gatekeeper looked at the car. He looked at Joe in the fruit hat. He opened the gate.

"Thank you for coming to the park, lady," said the gatekeeper to Joe.

The gatekeeper watched the yellow car speed off. He thought, *That driver with the funny hat looks very familiar.*

CHAPTER TWO
Another Prize for Joe

"Wheeee!" said Joe.

"SLOW DOWN! SAFETY FIRST!" Sparky shouted.

"Where do you want to go?"

Sparky thought and thought. "To my pond."

"You are always at your pond. Let's go somewhere different. How about that big building? It looks busy. It must be fun."

"Sitting on a warm rock can be fun," Sparky suggested.

"No," said Joe sadly. "Warm rocks are not fun."

Joe parked in front of the big building.

"Where are we?" Sparky asked.

"ATTENTION, CUSTOMERS: WELCOME TO THE TALL MALL!"

a loud voice announced.

Joe stretched his neck.

Sparky hid in his shell.

"What do we do here?"

Sparky said.

"FIND BIG SALES! SHOP TILL YOU DROP!"

said the voice.

"That sounds dangerous,"

Sparky whispered.

In the mall, Sparky
tried on a shirt.
It fit.

Joe tried on another shirt.
It almost fit.

Big &
TALL

Sparky got an orange helmet and safety goggles.

Joe got a surfboard, earmuffs, a basketball, two pairs of striped sports socks, a rack of candy, a SALE sign, sunglasses, and a brush.

"What is that thing that looks like your tail?" Sparky asked.

"It is a brush."

"Giraffes do not use brushes."

"Ones with well-brushed hair do," said Joe.

"Giraffes do not need well-brushed hair."

"Well, I am not your average Joe."

Sparky sighed. "I have shopped, and now I am ready to drop," he said.

Joe and Sparky followed
the other carts to the counter.
"Congratulations!" said
the man behind the counter.
"You are our one-millionth
customer. You win!
Your purchases are free!"

A band played.

Balloons floated.

Little pieces of paper fell from above.

"You won again, Joe! You won little

pieces of paper," Sparky said. "And they are

attacking me! HELP!"

On their way out, Joe and Sparky could
not believe what they saw.

"Look! There is another giraffe and
another turtle," Sparky said.

Joe and Sparky waved at them.

The other giraffe and turtle waved, too.

"They are nice," Joe said.

CHAPTER THREE
Welcome to Tasty Burger

"Why are all the other cars beeping at us?" Sparky asked.

"The cars are saying hello," Joe said, waving. "Hi, cars!"

"Thank goodness you are so smart about cars," Sparky said.

"Slam dunk! Look at that sign!" said Joe. "It has a picture of food."

"Is it a 'Do Not Feed the Animals' sort of sign?" asked Sparky.

"No. I think it is a 'Food for Everyone' sign."

Joe and Sparky saw other cars. The cars were parked next to small boxes. Joe and Sparky parked next to a small box.

"Welcome to Tasty Burger. Can I take your order?" the box asked.

"Yes. We would like some leaves," Joe said.

"And do not forget the bugs," Sparky said to Joe.

"Yes, and lots of bugs, please," Joe said.

The box was quiet.

"Hello, box?" Joe said.

"I do not understand. Would you like fries?" the box asked.

"Yes, we would like some flies," Sparky said.

They waited.

And waited.

Sparky looked at the car next to him.
It was red.

A girl on wheels rolled up to the red car.
She put a bag on a tray next to the red car's
window.

"Your lunch," said the girl to the red car.

"Our lunch? How nice!" Sparky said. He reached over and grabbed the bag. "Thank you for feeding the animals!"

The Super Flash 5000 sped away.

The girl rubbed her eyes. "I do not believe it!" she yelled.

"See, Sparky?" said Joe. "Even that person with little cars for feet cannot believe what a good driver I am."

Chapter Four
On the Road

"That food was not bad, but I am still hungry," Joe said.

"I miss the pond," Sparky said.

"We cannot go home yet, Sparky! We have many more places to see!"

First they watched cars ride upside
down. "Those are not good drivers,"
Sparky said.

After that they took a bath.

Then Joe stopped for a snack.

Soon the sun began to set.

"We have done everything," said Sparky proudly.

"Not everything," said Joe.

"But we have gone everywhere!"

"Not everywhere," said Joe.

"What could we have possibly missed?" Sparky asked.

"We have not sat on a warm rock. We have not gone to your pond."

"You are right, Joe!" said Sparky. "It is time to go back."

As the yellow car headed home, Sparky stared at its many buttons.

"What is this for?" he asked, pressing one.

"NEWS FLASH!" a strange voice yelled.

"THIS JUST IN...."

Sparky jumped.

"Oh, dear! Who is in the car with us?" Sparky asked.

"Nobody is in the car with us, silly," Joe said. "It is the car talking."

"A GIRAFFE AND A TURTLE HAVE BEEN SEEN CAUSING A HUBBUB AT THE..."

the voice continued.

"Oh, my!" Sparky said.

"Could it be the giraffe and turtle we saw at the store?" Joe asked.

"They seemed so nice," said Sparky.

Suddenly, **BOOM BANG!**

They were at their gate.

"Back again, lady?" the gatekeeper asked Joe. "We are about to close. I will let you in for free."

Joe and Sparky drove inside. They did not get far before they heard a sound. . . . *Put. Put. Phhhht.*

"Oh, no! The car stopped!" Sparky said.

"It must be taking a nap."

"What do we do?"

"We will leave it here for someone else. We do not need my car anymore," Joe said. "Cars are OK. But they would be better if they were not so small."

"And if they did not move," Sparky added.

"We can walk the rest of the way."

"Can you give me a lift?" Sparky asked.

"Always, my small, green friend." Joe said.

"We had a big day, Sparky, but it is good to be home. I do not think I care for shirts. They cover my lovely spots," said Joe.

"Yes, and those flies were not what I expected."

"Still, it is fun to try new things," Joe replied.

"It is. And trying new things made me love my old things even more," said Sparky. "Like my pond."

"Like my tall trees," said Joe.

"Like my warm rock."

"Like my watering hole."

"Like home."

"Like Wiggy."

"Who is Wiggy?" Sparky asked.

"My pet worm."

"Giraffes do not have pet worms."

"Some do," said Joe.

"You are a very different sort of giraffe."

"And you are a very different turtle,"
Joe said. "That is why I like you."

Sparky smiled. "Good night, Joe."

"Good night, my small, green friend."

On a nice warm rock, Sparky hid in his shell. ZZZZZZZZZ.

Not far away, Joe stretched his neck to see the world.

LEARN TO FLY